OKAPI
LOVES HIS
ZEBRA PANTS

All proceeds from this book go directly to okapi conservation.

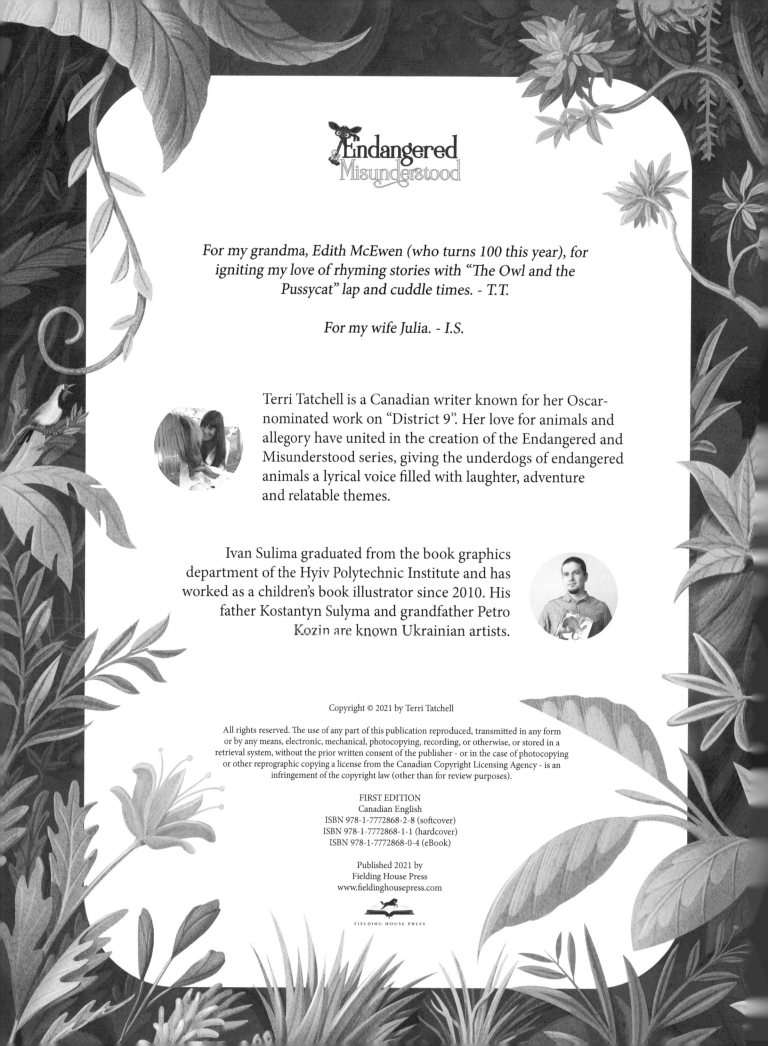

Endangered & Misunderstood

For my grandma, Edith McEwen (who turns 100 this year), for igniting my love of rhyming stories with "The Owl and the Pussycat" lap and cuddle times. - T.T.

For my wife Julia. - I.S.

Terri Tatchell is a Canadian writer known for her Oscar-nominated work on "District 9". Her love for animals and allegory have united in the creation of the Endangered and Misunderstood series, giving the underdogs of endangered animals a lyrical voice filled with laughter, adventure and relatable themes.

Ivan Sulima graduated from the book graphics department of the Hyiv Polytechnic Institute and has worked as a children's book illustrator since 2010. His father Kostantyn Sulyma and grandfather Petro Kozin are known Ukrainian artists.

FIRST EDITION
Canadian English
ISBN 978-1-7772868-2-8 (softcover)
ISBN 978-1-7772868-1-1 (hardcover)
ISBN 978-1-7772868-0-4 (eBook)

Published 2021 by
Fielding House Press
www.fieldinghousepress.com

FIELDING HOUSE PRESS

OKAPI
LOVES HIS
ZEBRA PANTS

Okapi loved his zebra pants
and wore them every day.
He never tried to take them off.
He wanted them to stay.

He really didn't think that they
were zebra pants at all.
He called them his okapi legs.
They helped to make him tall.

But then one day he met a chimp
who said, "I know a joke,
about a zebra's missing pants,
because the zipper broke."

He laughed, "I thought it was a tale,
but now I see it's true!
You stole those pants and put them on,
pretending they were you!"

That chimp was lost in laughter while
Okapi peered around,
and tugged and pulled at his striped legs,
then made a chuffing sound.

"I would not take a zebra's pants
because he'd be too cold.
These are my stripes upon my legs,
since I was one day old."

Okapi's friend, a Congo grey,
could hear them from her tree.
She flew straight down, right at the chimp,
and screeched, "Oh wait! I see!

You said that thing about his pants,
to make us notice you,
and say we liked your scary mask
and furry chin hair too.

Such silly ears that poke right out!
You really look a fright!
I'd lose that mask before it sticks
and scares you in the night."

The chimp stood up and touched his head.
And then he touched his ears.
"I always thought I looked quite nice.
I've looked this way for years!

It's not a mask, it's my real head!"
The tears were in his voice.
"I know my hair is rough and coarse.
I didn't have a choice.

This is the way that I was born.
I look just like my dad.
I merely meant to joke with you.
But now I feel quite sad."

Okapi smiled and told the chimp,
"It's Grey who's teasing you.
Your head is nice, as are your ears,
and all that chin hair too.

See, parrots are quite loyal friends,
they always have your back.
She's quick to come to my defense
in case of an attack."

The chimp, he saw, he'd been quite mean
and vowed to be more kind.
"I'm sorry that I laughed at you
and teased your striped behind.

But jokes aside, you simply must
check out a zebra herd.
Your legs, they are the same as theirs.
It really is absurd."

And just like that the chimp was gone.
But what he said, was not.
Okapi looked back at his legs,
and thought, "Well thanks a lot.

These legs that once belonged to me,
feel like they aren't mine now.
He says go find a zebra herd.
I'm just not quite sure how."

Well, Congo Grey saw her dear friend,
had taken this to heart.
So just before they slept that night,
she said, "You must be smart,

and see that chimp was poking fun,
because he didn't know,
a better way to make a friend.
So please just let it go!

But if you can't then rather shift
the focus of your mind.
Think why you like your gorgeous stripes
until your thoughts are kind."

That night Okapi tried to sleep.
He tossed and turned a lot.
And by the time the sun came up,
he'd thought and thought and thought.

Okapi had to learn the truth.
He couldn't let it be.
The only way to know for sure?
He'd go himself and see!

He didn't know where zebras lived.
Or if they all wore pants.
But what he knew was who to ask:
the wee bush el-e-phants.

He left right at the crack of dawn
and found them without trouble.
"My friends, I'm looking for a herd
whose bottoms are my double."

The elephants, all stared a while
then asked, "What do you mean?"
He told them what the chimp had said
then shared, "I've never seen

a zebra herd, or even one,
to know if this is true.
I hope that you can tell me where
to find just one or two."

"Sure, we can tell you where to go,
but wish that you would stay.
The zebras are beyond the trees.
There's danger out that way."

Okapi, he was stubborn and
had one thing on his mind.
And so, he thanked those elephants,
for being nice and kind.

Then set off right toward the sun.
It's what he had to do.
They yelled, "Be careful and watch out,
for things that might hurt you!"

And sure enough, their words were true.
The journey was alive,
with scary creatures everywhere.
If only Grey could drive!

There was a leopard in a tree.
Okapi knew to hide.
Then did his best to keep down wind
beneath a lion pride.

He made it through the dangers fine,
with fun stops on the way.
He splashed around with hippo friends,
and cooled off in their spray.

The nicest of gorillas said
Okapi looked unique.
Then took him to the jungle's edge,
"I'll show you what you seek."

She pointed out beyond the trees
and said, "I'll stop right here,
but if you head just past that hill,
the zebras will be near."

Okapi nearly lost his way
but in the end came right.
And when he found that zebra herd
he got a nasty fright.

Their legs had stripes just like he'd heard.
But so much more was true.
Stripes covered all the zebras' heads.
Their backs and bellies too.

"My dear friend Grey, why did we come?
I didn't need to know.
This is much worse than what I feared.
I think that we should go!"

But he stayed put and didn't move.
He watched that zebra herd.
Then turned to Grey and shook his head.
"This really is absurd.

I let that chimp get in my head
and make things seem so wrong.
My stripes are special as are theirs.
It's been true all along.

And now at last, I am quite thrilled,
to see I'm like the others.
Those zebras share my special stripes.
They're practically my brothers!"

As Grey reached down to stroke his cheek
she said, "My dear, that's right.
And look out way beyond them there,
a stork whose beak is bright.

That vivid red is just the same,
as my tail feathers are.
A red I thought was only mine!
It's good we came this far."

They spent the day with all new friends,
comparing heads and toes.

And at the end one thing was clear:
Not one was wearing clothes.

ENDANGERED AND MISUNDERSTOOD?

If an animal is endangered, its population is decreasing in numbers and the species is in danger of not existing anymore. The okapi (oh-KOP-ee) was discovered by Western science in 1901. We've barely had any time to appreciate and learn about okapis and they are already at risk of disappearing! Because they are so shy and only live deep in the tropical rainforest of the Democratic Republic of Congo, it is difficult to know exactly how many are left. Actual sightings are very rare so surveys are generally done by observing their dung! A lot is being done for okapi conservation in their homeland but many zoos worldwide are also participating in global breeding programs. Wouldn't it be amazing to meet a baby okapi!

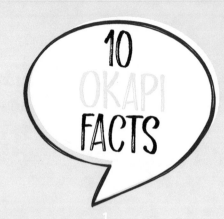

10 OKAPI FACTS

1. Okapis have oily fur so water rolls off keeping them dry.

2. Young okapis have a fringe of hair along their spine that disappears at one year of age.

3. Okapi is a ruminant, just like a cow. It swallows and regurgitates its herbivore diet for additional chewing several times.

4. Okapi calves don't defecate until 4 to 8 weeks old. Predators can't track them!

5. Other than man, leopards are the main predator of okapis.

6. Okapis mature at 2 to 3 years and live 20 to 30 years.

7. Okapis weigh 440 – 700 pounds.

8. Female okapis are bigger than male okapis.

9. Okapis mark their territory 3 ways. Spraying urine, rubbing their necks on trees and secreting a black tar-like substance from scent glands on their feet.

10. Males defend their territory from other males but let females pass through.

HOW TO DRAW THE OKAPI

5 AFRICAN GREY FACTS

1. African grey parrots are endangered due to poaching for the pet trade and destruction of their habitat.

2. African grey parrots have the mental and emotional intelligence of a 5-year-old child!

3. African grey parrots can mimic human speech, identify shapes and colours, learn number sequences, ask unprompted questions and hold entire conversations.

4. They can live up to 80 years!

5. Rescued African grey parrots are so smart they help their humans look after them. They ask for apples, corn, water and to be put to bed.

HOW TO DRAW THE AFRICAN GREY PARROT

Endangered Misunderstood

FIVE WAYS TO HELP ENDANGERED ANIMALS

3

Learn about endangered animals in your own environment and research ways to help them.

Help your parents learn how to make your home wildlife friendly.

Be creative! Use art and stories to help introduce endangered animals to friends and family.

Reuse and recycle whenever you can!

Share what you are doing with us so we can share and inspire others!

For complimentary songs, story time videos, activities and more visit:
endangeredandmisunderstood.com

Printed in the USA
CPSIA information can be obtained
at www.ICGtesting.com
LVHW071327230823
R17862000004B/R178620PG755608LVX00001B/1